AHOY THERE!

Pirates Can Listen

Published in paperback in 2017

Text © Hodder and Stoughton 2017
Illustrations© Mike Gordon

Wayland
Carmelite House
50 Victoria Embankment
London EC4Y 0DZ

Wayland Australia
Level 17/207 Kent Street
Sydney, NSW 2000

Commissioning editor: Victoria Brooker
Creative design: Basement68

A catalogue record for this book is
available from the British Library.
Dewey number: 823.9'2-dc23

ISBN 978 0 7502 9625 0
Ebook ISBN 978 0 7502 9626 7

Printed in China

10 9 8 7 6 5 4 3 2 1

Wayland is a division of
Hachette Children's Group,
an Hachette UK company.
www.hachette.co.uk

AHOY THERE!

Pirates Can Listen

Written by
Tom Easton

Illustrated by
Mike Gordon

WAYLAND

The crew of the *Golden Duck* were very excited. They were in Port Pegleg and their pockets were bulging with treasure.

"Now listen carefully," Captain Cod told the pirates. "Watch out for my old enemy, Captain Blackears, and his Horrid Pirates. I saw their ship, the *Bad Dog*, moored on the other side of the harbour."

But no one was listening to the captain as he
spoke. "Remember, keep your treasure
well-hidden," he said. "Otherwise
the Horrid Pirates will steal it."

"Polly, you look after the ship,"
the Captain said. But Polly wasn't paying
attention either. She had seen a big sign
in town which read 'Cracker Factory'.

As soon as the gangplank was in place, the pirates rushed off into the town. Sam and Nell headed for the shops. Davy and Pete headed for the ice cream parlour. And Polly?
Well, Polly wanted a cracker to eat.

"What about this dress?" Nell said, showing Sam one with skulls and crossbones on it.

"It's really expensive!" Sam said, his eyes
bulging at the price tag.
Nell shrugged. "That's OK. I have loads
of treasure," she said, slapping a big bag
of gold coins on the counter.

At the ice cream parlour, Davy and Pete had just ordered the biggest ice cream sundaes in the shop.
  Pete was staring at a pirate captain sitting at a table. The Captain's ears were as black as tar.
  "I haven't seen you lads in here before," the pirate captain said.

"We just arrived this morning," Pete said. "On the *Golden Duck*."

"That's Captain Cod's ship, isn't it?" the captain asked, rubbing one of his ears.

"Yes," replied Davy, with his mouth full of ice cream. "Why do you ask?"

Meanwhile, poor Polly Parrot had been disappointed to find the factory made the wrong sort of crackers.

The exploding kind.
She sat on the weathervane on top of the town hall and went to sleep.

Captain Cod had been shopping. He'd bought
a new peg leg and an enormous hat. He wandered
back to the ship, humming a shanty.
On the way, he had to hide in an alley as two
Horrid Pirates ran out of a dress shop,
each carrying a bag of gold.

More Horrid Pirates came rushing out of the ice cream parlour.

"Stop, thief!" someone called. Captain Cod crawled past so they wouldn't see him.

No-one was at the ship when the Captain returned.

He tutted and looked at his watch.

Polly Parrot woke with a start as a group of cackling Horrid Pirates clattered along the street below.

"Let's get this treasure back to the *Bad Dog*," said Captain Blackears.

Polly squawked in alarm and flapped her way back to the ship.

"Calm down, Polly" said Captain Cod when she arrived. "Tell me everything that's happened."
So Polly did. The captain listened very carefully.

Four pirates trudged back to the *Golden Duck*.
"I wish the Captain had told us about
the Horrid Pirates," Pete said.
"I wish he'd told us to keep quiet
about the treasure," Nell added.
"I'm hungry," Davy said.

The Captain was waiting for them back at the ship. All the pirates started shouting at once.

"They took our gold," Nell said.

"What are we going to do?" Sam pleaded.

"Why didn't you tell us about the Horrid Pirates?" Pete demanded.

"Is there any food?" Davy asked.

"LISTEN!" the Captain shouted.
Everyone stopped talking.
"The reason you're in this mess
is that you didn't listen to me."

There was a flapping sound overhead. "Polly!" they all cried. The parrot dropped a package on the deck. Nell unwrapped it.

"Crackers!" she said.

"Great," said Davy. "I'm starving."

"Not those sort of crackers," Nell said.

"These are the exploding kind."

"Polly and I know exactly where the stolen treasure is," the Captain said, a glint in his eye. "And we know exactly how we're going to get it back." He told them the plan and, this time, the crew listened.

That night, when all the good folk of Port Pegleg were safely tucked in their beds, the quiet was broken by a CRACK and a BANG and a POP and a BOOM down at the harbour.

The Horrid Pirates woke in alarm and rushed down the gangplank to investigate the noise. They didn't notice, in the confusion, that the *Golden Duck* had slipped quietly along the other side of their ship.

"Now!" whispered the Captain.
They leapt aboard the *Bad Dog*
and snatched the treasure bags.

"Hey!" roared Captain Blackears,
as he saw what was happening.
"I"ll get you, Cod!"

But the Horrid Pirates were too late. Captain Cod's crew sprang back on board the *Golden Duck* and cast off. They sailed out of the harbour, the Horrid Pirates shouting rude names after them.

"What are they shouting?" Sam asked. The Captain clapped his hands over Sam's ears and said, "Maybe this one time it's better NOT to listen."

NOTES FOR PARENTS AND TEACHERS

Pirates to the Rescue

The books in the 'Pirates to the Rescue' series are designed to help children recognise the virtues of good manners and behaviour. Reading these books will show children that their actions have a real effect on people around them, helping them to recognise what is right and wrong, and to think about what to do when faced with difficult choices.

Ahoy There!

'Ahoy There!' is intended to be an engaging and enjoyable read for children aged 4-7. The book will help children recognise why it's important to listen and pay attention.

When Captain Cod gives the pirates advice on how to behave on shore, he is trying to keep them safe. Unfortunately, the pirates allow themselves to be distracted by thoughts of the fun that awaits them. After they lose their gold, they complain that the captain didn't warn them of the dangers. To make matters worse, they interrupt the captain when he's trying to help them. In contrast, when he learns of his crew's predicament, the captain listens carefully to Polly to get the information he needs to form a plan. By distracting the Horrid Pirates with too much noise the captain saves the day.

Learning to listen is a vital skill used in all areas of life. Children need to be able to listen carefully in order to successfully complete tasks and keep safe at school, at home and out and about. Being able to listen effectively will help children to learn good manners as well as how to interact with others — skills that don't come naturally to all children. Listening is a social skill and enables communication and exchanging of ideas.

It's difficult for children to remember to listen. Especially when there are so many distractions. We are all surrounded by sound and sights and learning to focus on the important things can take time. Help children to listen carefully.

Active listening requires people to learn to judge when to speak and when to remain silent. It is a vital aspect of any team-based activity. Without listening we cannot make sense of, assess, or respond to what we hear.

Remember to listen to children and make a show of it. Children imitate behaviour and if you don't show you are listening, then they will not consider listening to be important.

Suggested follow-up activities

Talk about the events in the book. Ask children to Identify the times when the pirates didn't listen, and when they did.

Play listening games. Fill a bag with objects that make a distinctive sound and ask children to guess what each one is.

Read out loud regularly to children so they become used to the rhythms and patterns of your voice. Change the names in a familiar story and ask children to identify what was different.

Make eye contact with children when you give advice or instruction. Get down to the child's level to make sure you have their full attention.

Listing things aids memory. Play memory games, such as "I went to the shop and bought an apple..."

BOOKS TO SHARE

Everybody Matters: A First Look at Respect
by Pat Thomas and Lesley Harker (Wayland, 2014)

Everyone deserves respect, whether it is by being treated fairly
or by not being discriminated against because they are different.
This book shows how you can earn respect, by being polite,
honest or listening to others.

Monkey Needs to Listen (Behaviour Matters)
by Sue Graves (Watts, 2011)

Monkey is so excited about a go-kart race that he doesn't listen
to any of the instructions. He doesn't stop to check his kart and he
nearly ruins the race for all the animals. Can Monkey learn to listen
and pay attention or will the race be abandoned for good?

The Worst Day of My Life Ever:
My Story about listening
and following instructions
by Julia Cook

RJ has a bad day. He's late,
gets into trouble for not handing
in homework and makes a mess at
home. With his mum's help, he learns
that his problems are happening
because he's not listening. This
story shows how listening can
turn bad days into good days.